*For C.H., A.K., and N.M., with love*
~ S. J.

*For Greg (a lifelong friend), Agata, and their*
*perfect little present, Zosia; born Nov. 2, 2015*
~ C. P.

tiger tales
5 River Road, Suite 128, Wilton, CT 06897
Published in the United States 2016
Originally published in Great Britain 2016
by Little Tiger Press
Text by Stella J. Jones
Text copyright © 2016 Little Tiger Press
Illustrations copyright © 2016 Caroline Pedler
ISBN-13: 978-1-68010-036-5
ISBN-10: 1-68010-036-X
Printed in China
LTP/1400/1445/0216
10 9 8 7 6 5 4 3 2 1

For more insight and activities, visit us at www.tigertalesbooks.com

# The Perfect Present

by Stella J. Jones • Illustrated by Caroline Pedler

tiger tales

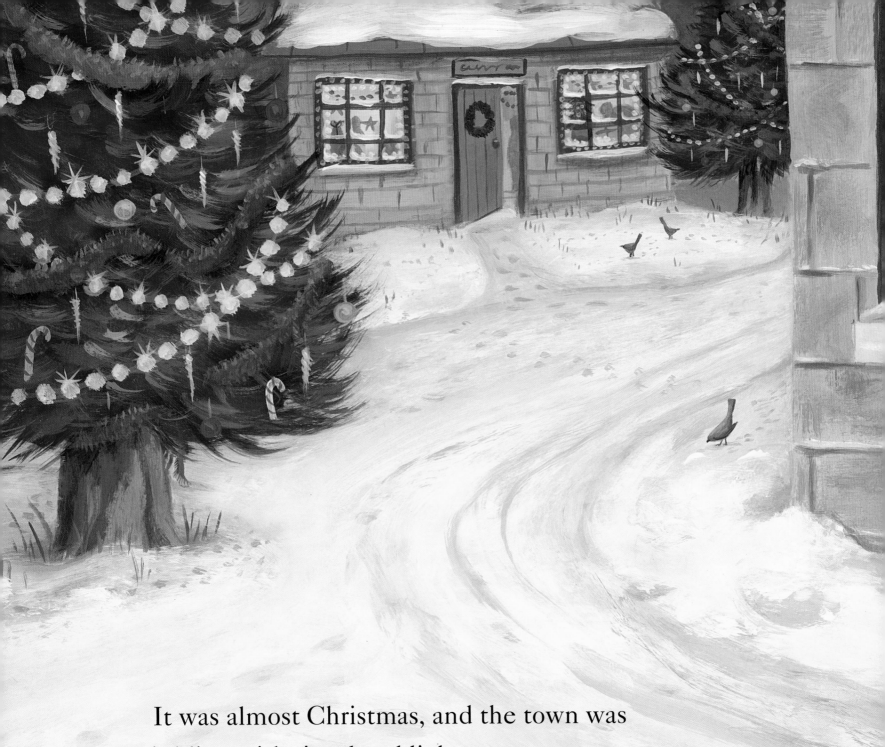

It was almost Christmas, and the town was
twinkling with tinsel and lights.

"This is the BEST time of year!" cheered Bobby,
zooming along on his scooter.

"Faster, faster!" called Bella, pedaling up beside him.
"Or we'll miss the lighting of the Christmas tree!"

"Three, two, one, hooray!"
everyone cried as the tree
sparkled to life.
"One more night until Santa
comes!" smiled Bella,
squeezing Bobby's paw.

"One last day for Christmas shopping!"
grinned Bobby. "See you later!"
He hopped on his scooter and rushed off
to buy Bella the perfect gift.

The shelves at Hattie Hardwick's shop were filled with beautiful things, but nothing was just right for Bella.

"Oh, no," sighed Bobby.

Then something bright and red caught his eye.

"A flag for Bella's trike!" he gasped. "Bella would love that!"

We SWAP
OLD for
NEW!

But Bobby didn't have enough money.
"This is awful!" he frowned. "What will I do?"

"Don't worry," said Hattie gently. "Is there something you'd like to swap for the flag?"

Bobby thought hard and looked down at his battered scooter. Could he possibly part with it?

"I can swap this," he said bravely, handing the scooter to Hattie.

"Bella will love her present,"
Bobby told himself as he
looked up at his scooter
in the window.

But he couldn't help feeling a little sad
as he padded slowly home through the
crowds of busy Christmas shoppers.

Across town, it didn't take Bella long to find
the perfect present for Bobby.
"That's it!" she cried, staring at the
brightest, shiniest bell in the shop window.
"I'll get Bobby that bell for his scooter."

She rushed into the shop,
but she didn't have enough
money, either!

"This is terrible," sighed Bella.

**NEW for OLD! Why not SWAP?**

Suddenly, she spotted a sign behind the counter. It said:

New for old! Why not swap?

"What could I give?" Bella pondered. Then she had an idea. "I can swap my trike!" she told the shopkeeper.

Bella sniffled a little as she left her trusty trike behind.

But she soon cheered up when she thought about how much Bobby would love his bell.

After they'd warmed up with Christmas hot chocolate, the siblings raced off to wrap their gifts.

"You're going to love your present!" called Bobby as he snipped and folded the wrapping paper.

"Not as much as you'll like yours!" replied Bella, tying a bow.

But as they slept, scooters and trikes whooshed and zipped through their dreams—and they were always just out of reach.

"Merry Christmas!" Bobby and Bella cried
as the sun peeked through the curtains.
   "Ready?" asked Bobby.
   "Set!" cried Bella.
   "Unwrap!" they shouted together.

Bobby couldn't believe his eyes!

"A bell for my scooter!" he gasped.

"And a flag for my trike!" squealed Bella.

"This is the best present ever!"

And then they remembered . . . .

"But I . . . I swapped my scooter for your flag," sniffed Bobby.
"And I swapped my trike for your bell!" gulped Bella.

Bella gave Bobby a hug.
"I don't mind that I don't
have my trike," she said.
"I still have you."

"You really are the best sister
ever," smiled Bobby.

"Let's open our presents from Santa," suggested Bobby. "That will cheer us up."

He reached under the tree and pulled out two packages. There was a note that read:

Dear Bobby and Bella,
I know what kind and thoughtful little bears you have both been, so my elves have been working on something very special for you.
Merry Christmas!
Love, Santa

"What could it be?" wondered Bella as she tore off the paper.

"I don't believe it!" she exclaimed. "It's . . . it's my trike! It's fixed!"

"And look! My scooter!" added Bobby. "It looks brand new! Thank you, Santa!"

With the bell and flag in place, there was only
one thing left to do.

"Race you to the pond and back!"
called Bella happily.

"Ready, set, GO!" laughed Bobby.

And the two rushed out into the snowy Christmas day.